TOMMY BLUE AND REX IN GIGANTIC DANGER

JANE CARTER

First published 2024
by Rowanvale Books Ltd
The Gate
Keppoch Street
Roath
Cardiff
CF24 3JW
www.rowanvalebooks.com

A CIP catalogue record for this book is available from the British Library.
ISBN: 978-1-83584-036-8

For Jake and Pip – the original Tommy Blue and Rex.

Dear Reader, this story is set near Abergavenny, South Wales, right at the tip of the Skirrid mountain. It's an ancient place, full of magic and excitement, where strange creatures hide in the shadows of the woodlands. If you look up and see a puff of smoke in the sky, it might be coming from a cottage fireplace, or it could be the smoky breath of a sleeping Welsh dragon.

REX

CHAPTER 1

Tommy Blue lives with his mum and dad and his much-loved dog Rex on a small farm on the Skirrid mountain.

Their flock of sheep looks like tiny dots of candyfloss on the fields high above the farmhouse. The sounds of their bleats as they call to one another can be heard from far away.

The only other animals on the farm are the chickens, who spend their days scratching for worms in the garden. They lay their golden-yolked prizes in lots of secret places, and Mum spends ages hunting them out each morning for the family's breakfast.

The farmhouse has a red-tiled roof with a large, brick chimney to one side. There are two bay windows on each of the two floors, and right in the centre of the house is a big, oak door with a brass knocker in the shape of a fire-breathing dragon. It's the sort of home a child might draw and looks for all the world like a giant doll's house.

In front of the house is a square lawn with three round flowerbeds full of rose bushes. Each summer they light up the garden with their bright red blooms. In the corner of the lawn stands a flagpole bearing the Welsh flag with its magnificent dragon.

Tommy Blue and Rex are best friends and have been from the moment Rex, then a tiny black puppy, arrived just a week after Tommy Blue's first birthday, nine years ago. He was a present from Nell, the beautiful fairy who lives deep in the magical Skirrid woodlands with her band of followers: the Tatties. She gave the puppy to Tommy Blue's parents when she learnt that their child would never walk. She is a true friend to all who live on the mountain, and a terrible enemy to those who might hurt them.

Rex isn't all black. There's a bit of white on his head that's shaped like a crown. That's how he got his name: 'Rex' is an old word for king. A good name for such a special dog.

The two chums are very tired. The last year has been jam-packed with a number of hair-raising antics, and they're looking forward to a few quiet weeks together at home this summer. Little do they know that life will be anything but quiet.

Adventures are coming.

CHAPTER 2

Our story begins one warm July morning. Tommy Blue is at the kitchen table eating sausage, egg and toast.

Tommy Blue is big for his age and still growing fast. Today he's proudly wearing a brand-new football shirt that Mum gave him yesterday when he got home from school. His last one, which he loved and wore every day, had become far too snug.

He's watching his mother as she puts the final touches to the Victoria sponge cake she bakes every year to mark the start of the summer holidays.

Mum is short and plump with bright red hair that hangs in thick, springy curls to her shoulders. She has a round, soft face with the warmest of smiles, and when she's home in the kitchen, she always smells of baking and rose petals. Today she's wearing her favourite cotton apron, covered in yellow daffodils.

Mum carries the cake, thick with butter icing and homemade strawberry jam, to the table, sliding it off the cooling rack and onto a china cake stand.

It's the start of Mum's holiday as well. She works in the village blacksmith's where she makes fairies and goblins from old bits of scrap metal. On the first

Tuesday of every month, she takes these beautiful pieces of art to Abergavenny market, where they sell like hotcakes.

‘How’s your breakfast?’ she asks Tommy Blue. ‘I found these eggs first thing this morning, so they should be extra scrummy.’

‘Oh, they are,’ says Tommy Blue. ‘Thanks, Mum.’

Then he asks, ‘Mum, where’s Rex?’

‘I let him out into the garden an hour ago after he’d gobbled down a huge bowl of dog food. I’ve never known an animal with such a gigantic appetite. I just saw him trying to round up those daft chickens. I don’t know why he bothers – they take no notice of him!'

She looks at Tommy Blue and gives a quick smirk.

'Poor Rex,' she says. 'Those hens are so naughty. They know he only wants to play, but they act as if he doesn't eggs-ist. Ha-ha!'

The two of them are still laughing at Mum's joke when Rex comes bounding in through the open kitchen door and jumps onto the chair next to Tommy Blue, just as the boy takes a large bite of sausage.

'Ith hadff a fhunny dreampt.'

Rex and Mum look at Tommy Blue curiously.

Taking a great slurp from his mug of sweet, milky tea, he swallows down his food.

'Sorry, Mum,' he says. 'I know you don't like me speaking with my mouth full. I said, I had a funny dream. Rex, you were in it. We were fighting a fierce monster, and you were speaking to me in French. It gave me such a shock it woke me up.'

Rex looks at his best friend for a moment. Then…

'How utterly ridiculous,' he says. 'You know I only speak the King's English, with the odd Welsh word here and there. What an amazing dream, though. All I ever dream about is chasing chickens.'

CHAPTER 3

Dear Reader, did I tell you that Rex is a magical dog? No? How silly of me. Rex is a very special dog. He can talk, but only to the Blue family, and he can do other things, but more on that later. Read on – you're in for a great surprise.

Tommy Blue takes a final bite of his fry-up and, still chewing, spreads peanut butter on his toast. Rex leans closer to Tommy Blue, his nose only millimetres away from the nutty, buttery yumminess.

'Hey, paws off, Rex. I'm starving – and I know Mum has already fed you,' Tommy Blue says with a laugh, tickling Rex's ears and giving him a quick peck on the snout.

Rex wags his tail madly.

Tommy Blue bites into the toast, leaving the imprint of his teeth on the thick layer of peanut butter. Rex leans even closer, a small dribble of drool gently dripping down from the corner of his mouth.

Tommy Blue puts the toast down and uses both hands to try and push Rex away, but the dog places his snout onto the boy's cheek, trying to distract him with doggy kisses.

'Oooh your nose is cold and wet.' Tommy Blue laughs, finally managing to gently push Rex onto the floor.

A moment later, Dad comes in from the farmyard.

'Something smells good,' he says, smiling at Mum as he takes off his wellies and leaves them outside the kitchen door. Then, tucking the legs of his overalls into his long woollen socks and taking off his baseball cap, he makes his way towards the table.

'Sorry I'm late,' he says, 'but I was counting the sheep and kept falling asleep.'

Tommy Blue looks up at Dad and chuckles. His father is always full of fun and loves being silly. Dad is tall and thin with just a small band of dark, curly hair around his bald head. Like Mum, he has a kind and gentle face, a twinkle in his eye, and a smile that goes from ear to ear.

As Dad comes further into the kitchen, his glasses steam up with the heat from the room, and Tommy Blue laughs as his dad pretends to crash blindly into the table, arms stretched out, aiming for the cake.

'Hands off,' cries Mum as she playfully swats Dad away with the edge of her apron. 'You'll have to wait. I'm not cutting the cake till after lunch.'

Dad sits at the table opposite Tommy Blue, and Mum brings

him a couple of soft-boiled eggs with a piece of buttered toast, cut into soldiers. Taking off his glasses to wipe away the steam, he looks at his son.

'Have you heard about the farmer who bred a three-legged chicken?'

'No,' says Tommy Blue. 'Why did he do that?'

'He thought it would stop his three sons fighting over who got a leg when they had a chicken dinner.'

'Gosh' says Tommy Blue. 'How clever of him. Was the chicken extra tasty?'

'Nobody knows,' says Dad, his mouth twitching as he tries not to smile. ‘No one’s ever been able to catch it.’

Tommy Blue bursts into a fit of giggles, and Rex, who loves the tinkling sound of his master’s laugh, tips his head back and howls with glee.

Mum, on the other hand, doesn’t see what’s so funny.

‘I don’t get it,’ she says.

‘Will one of you tell her?’ asks Dad.

But Tommy Blue and Rex can’t speak for laughing, and so Dad turns to Mum.

‘The chicken has three legs, so it can run really fast, much faster than the farmer. That’s why he’s never been able to catch it. Get it?'

'I suppose,' she says with a sigh. 'You and your silly dad jokes!'

She goes over to Tommy Blue and gently strokes his mass of dark curls.

'This needs a jolly good cut,' she says. 'I'll take you to the barber's tomorrow morning.'

Tommy Blue grins up at Mum through his round, thick-lensed glasses. He loves trips into the village with his mother because she always takes him to the sweet shop. She bends down to give her son a kiss. Then, peering into his face, she frowns.

‘Oh, my word,’ she cries. ‘Your glasses are very dirty. How do you manage to see out of them? I think you left your cleaning cloth near the television. Now, off you go and give them a good clean.’

Tommy Blue steers his electric wheelchair into the family room, Rex trotting by his side.

As they go, they chat about all the fun things they’ve got planned for the days ahead, unaware of the terror to come.

CHAPTER 4

In the family room, Tommy Blue cleans his glasses, and the pair settle down in front of the telly.

As luck would have it, their favourite cartoon has just started. It's about Prince George and his brave and loyal dog – Bruce. Like Rex, the cartoon animal is large and black and, with the prince, is always getting into scrapes. Every episode is full of action and danger, but each one ends with the prince and Bruce beating a different enemy.

They watch as their heroes bravely fight a gang of nasty sea monsters that are causing trouble in a small fishing village.

At the end of the show, Rex is feeling sleepy after a morning chasing chickens. He snuggles close to Tommy Blue's chair and closes his eyes. He's almost nodding off when suddenly, he jumps up. He looks up at Tommy Blue.

'Have you farted?' he says sharply.

'No, I haven't,' says Tommy Blue. 'But you're right,' he says. 'There's a nasty stink coming from somewhere. What do you think it is?'

Rex runs over to the open window, sticks his head outside,

and takes a deep sniff. When he looks back into the room, his face is serious.

'The air is thick with the stench of monstrous giants,' he says. 'They're back.'

***

Giants had come to the mountain last year, causing trouble wherever they went and scaring the villagers.

There had been three of them, and the largest and most horrible one was the leader. The children called him Ragnar. He stood over ten metres tall and was dressed in a coat made from the dark brown skins of several large bears. These were roughly sewn together and tied around his waist with a belt made from two vast crocodile skins. He used a tree trunk, stripped of its branches, as a club.

His brother Rollo wore five moth-eaten tiger furs that he'd wrapped around his large, round belly. To stop the furs from falling down and uncovering Rollo's great, spotty bum, he'd tied the five tails together. Then, to hold everything in place, he'd taken a tail and clamped it between the sharp teeth of one of the tiger skulls. From far away (which is the distance you want to be from a giant), it looked like the animal was chewing on a foul-tasting snack.

The third giant, their sister Oda, had a dress made from three buffalo hides, tied at her neck and waist with living water snakes plaited into thick belts. Only girl giants wear these belts. The serpents wriggled and hissed around her, but she knew she was safe from attack. These snakes only sink their fangs into the extra smelly skin of boy giants.

Rollo and Oda were both a head shorter than their brother Ragnar, but twice as wide.

All three were barefooted and their large, deformed feet had left huge prints in the ground that still filled with water when it rained. Like all giants, they had green-coloured skin that matched their broken, tombstone-like teeth, and they were totally hairless. Their bodies were covered in large, pus-filled spots and crusty warts as big as dinner plates. They were all very ugly, and smelt strongly of the damp, rotting swamps where they lived.

If they've broken through the spells and are back on the mountain, Tommy Blue and Rex need to defeat them again, and quickly.

CHAPTER 5

Tommy Blue grips the joystick on his electric wheelchair, and together the friends race to the kitchen.

Tommy Blue quickly tells Mum and Dad what's happened before he and Rex hurry out into the farmyard, towards the workshop. Taking the remote control from the arm of the wheelchair, he points it at the workshop's large barn doors. Slowly, they begin to slide open. As soon as they can, the pair rush inside and get straight to work.

Sitting on an old, cast-iron table in the middle of the room is a globe-shaped object the size of a beach ball. This is the Giant Tracker, which was created using powerful magic by Nell when the giants had first come to the Skirrid looking for tasty treats.

The globe is made from a special rock that fell from the sky and landed near Abergavenny hundreds of years ago. The mountain's houses, farmland, woods, and streams are all clearly marked on it. Inside, it is hollow and there's a light that, once switched on, casts a map of the landscape onto the workshop ceiling. If giants are present on the mountain, they show up as dots, their position clearly marked.

Tommy Blue steers his chair up to the table and flicks a small switch on the base of the Tracker. The pair wait close by, wondering what they'll see. Rex stands by Tommy Blue's side, resting his head on the arm of the wheelchair. He looks up at his best friend.

'What are you thinking? Could the giants be back?' he asks Tommy Blue.

'Gosh, I dunno. Hopefully there's nothing there and what you smelt was something else. Perhaps it was simply Farmer Powell spreading muck on his fields.'

Rex decides not to be cross at his powerful sense of smell being doubted. Instead, he stands quietly, slowly wagging his tail as he allows Tommy Blue to stroke his head and scratch his ears.

The seconds feel like hours, but soon they see what they've been dreading – there are three dots on the mountainside, heading towards the village. Tommy Blue's hand is shaking as he takes a small pen-like object from the side of the Tracker and points it at the first dot.

When he clicks a button on the top of the pen, the picture on the ceiling disappears and is replaced by the terrifying face of Ragnar.

Tommy Blue swallows down a shout of fear. He clicks on the other dots and soon discovers that Rollo and Oda have once again joined their brother. He knows what they're after and he needs to warn the villagers. There's not a moment to lose.

'Yikes!' cries Rex. 'This is terrible. How on earth did those three get back on the Skirrid? We need to get to the village and move the children to safety before they're captured and taken back to the Land of the Giants – never to be seen again.'

'Rex, you're right. We need to get the chariot.'

Dear Reader, did you know that giants love eating children? They are by far a giant's favourite meal, especially when sandwiched between two giant-sized pieces of white bread, with just a dash of fresh bogey.

CHAPTER 6

Quickly, Tommy Blue heads towards the back wall of the workshop, where a large, bulky object is covered by an old, dusty sheet. Tommy Blue grabs one corner of the cloth and pulls.

A huge cloud of dust rises in the air and quickly settles to reveal a small, steel chariot. Created by Mum in her workshop, it's decorated with a beautiful painting of a terrifying, fire-breathing dragon. The beast looks as if it's in flight, with wings outstretched, chasing a deadly enemy.

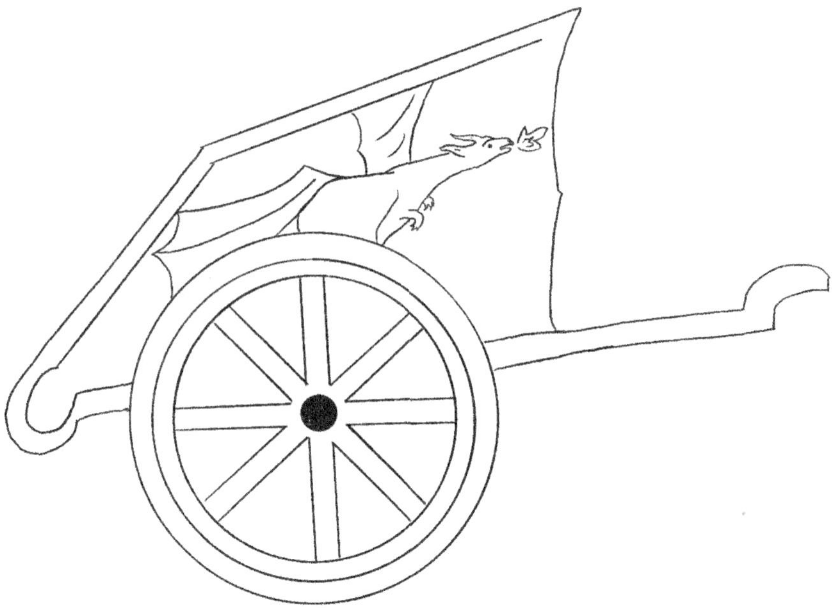

On each side of the chariot are matching, wooden-spoked wheels, and inside is a special seat for Tommy Blue, wide enough for him to sit in comfortably. It has a safety harness, like the ones used by racing car drivers, to keep him from falling out when the chariot travels at speed.

There's also a control panel, in front of Tommy Blue's seat, that has a smaller version of the Giant Tracker plus two large buttons. One is shaped like a telephone.

In front of the chariot are two long wooden poles with lots of straps. Tommy Blue first uses these to harness Rex, before pushing himself out of his chair and into the body of the chariot. Once safely in place, Tommy Blue presses the telephone-shaped button and speaks to Rex.

'I'm in,' he cries. 'Let's go!'

Setting off at a run, Rex pulls the chariot out of the workshop. They race through the farmyard to the open kitchen door, stopping only briefly for Tommy Blue to tell his parents what they've seen. Then the two friends speed off. They head across the garden to the narrow lane that leads to the village, scattering squawking hens and feathers everywhere.

Mum and Dad run outside, watching them go.

'Good luck, my darling boy!' shouts Mum.

Back inside, Dad runs upstairs to fetch a suitcase while his wife starts getting warm clothes and blankets together, ready to pack. Before they leave, she grabs a couple of freshly baked loaves of bread and a packet of butter and fills three flasks with sweet, milky tea. Then they jump into Dad's old van and follow Tommy Blue and Rex as they race to warn the villagers.

Rex moves like a bullet. He runs so fast that Tommy Blue, safe inside his chariot, feels like he's flying.

Within minutes, they're outside the grocery shop where old Mr Jones lives. Mr Jones is the village's Giant Warden. It's his job to warn the villagers when the giants attack and lead the families to safety. As soon as the chariot comes to a stop, Rex barks out the special giant alert signal – three woofs followed by one long howl.

A minute later, the door flings open and Mr Jones races out

to see them, knocking over the fruit and vegetable stand that sits in front of the shop. Oranges, apples, leeks, and potatoes spill out across the pavement, but Mr Jones just kicks them aside as he runs up to Tommy Blue.

‘Is it another attack?’ he cries. ‘Are they really back again?’

He’s as white as a sheet and looks very scared. Tommy Blue guesses he must have got dressed in a hurry this morning, as the old man’s thick, white hair looks like it needs a good

brush and his pyjama bottoms can be seen poking out from below his brown, woollen trousers.

'Yes, they're back,' says Tommy Blue. 'There are three of them, the same ones as before, and they're running up the mountain. We need to get all the children and their parents to the Giant Shelter before those brutes come anywhere near the village. Mr Jones, you need to sound the alarm.'

'Righty-ho,' says Mr Jones as he hurries to his flat above the shop.

Leaning out of the front bedroom window, he takes a deep breath and blows with all his might down a long, straight horn that's twisted into a sharp point. The children think it's a unicorn horn, but in fact it's made from the tusk of a narwhal.

These strange and beautiful creatures once lived in the waters off South Wales, many years ago when the seas were colder. The horn makes a musical yet chilling sound as Mr Jones blows into it.

The noise travels across the village. The families know what to do, and it's not long before they can be seen running towards Tommy Blue and Rex. Some of the children are clutching teddies and dollies, while others run holding tightly onto comfort blankets. Each child looks alarmed, running ahead of their frightened parents.

Soon, all the villagers, including Mum and Dad, have arrived outside Mr Jones's shop.

Suddenly, a small, trembling voice rings out. 'Tommy Blue, my sister's not here. Please don't leave her behind.'

Tommy Blue sees Jack, a little boy of about seven, covered in great splashes of mud and wearing shorts and a T-shirt over his thin frame. He's famous for climbing, and falling, from the many oaks in the village, and his skinny legs and arms are covered in cuts and bruises. Everyone in the village knows him and his twin sister.

Jack and Gilly are the naughtiest children in school by far! The head teacher, Mrs Jenkins, is always having to tell them off for being cheeky, and they spend at least one day a week in trouble for being rude. Their parents have nicknamed them the Terrible Two.

Their latest prank involved opening a full tin of tar and covering themselves from head to toe in the oozy goop. Their mum and dad have been trying for the last couple of days to get the tar off, but patches still remain behind their ears and knees.

Tommy Blue stares at Jack. He's worried because the pair are rarely apart, and he's never seen the child look so frightened.

'Do you know where she is, Jack?' he asks.

'Yes, she's at the river catching fish,' says Jack. 'I was at home getting us some jam sandwiches and bottles of pop.'

'Don't worry,' says Tommy Blue. 'We'll get her. You go with the others to the Giant Shelter. Rex and I will bring her there.'

As the villagers leave, Tommy Blue turns the chariot around and races off to save the child.

What they see when they get to the river almost turns their blood to ice. On the other side of the bank is Gilly. With her blonde hair tied into bunches and her jeans and T-shirt stained with grass and mud, she's standing on a large rock, moving her net slowly through the water. She's listening to loud music on her headphones, so she can't hear the three large shapes racing towards her.

GIANTS!

CHAPTER 7

As Rex and Tommy Blue watch in horror, the giants race towards Gilly. Large splashes of spit spray off their chins as they look forward to the sweetness of the meal ahead.

Tommy Blue tries to cry 'GILLY!' but the word sticks in his throat. He feels so afraid he can't move, watching silently as Ragnar swoops down and picks up the child. Rex is rooted to the spot in shock.

Dear Reader, do you find it strange that Tommy Blue and

Rex are so scared? After all, they have fought and beaten these rotten giants before. Are you thinking that they aren't acting like brave fighters? Did you know that real courage comes when you take action, even when you're afraid? Keep reading, and judge for yourself the true bravery of Tommy Blue and Rex.

Ragnar opens his mouth wide and is about to pop Gilly in when he stops, a look of horror on his face. He brings her tiny body up to his ugly, wart-covered nose and sniffs.

'Yuck – what a pong!' he shouts.

He turns towards Oda and Rollo.

‘My lunch stinks,’ he says angrily. ‘She’ll need a wash in the swamp before I can eat her. Come on, you two, we need to get home. We’ll come back later for the other children. Hopefully, they won’t smell so nasty.’

Throwing his club to the ground in anger, he tightens his grip on Gilly, closing his fingers around her struggling body, trapping her from escape.

The three giants, unaware of Tommy Blue and Rex watching on, whoop with delight. The sound is both ear-splitting and stomach-turning in its awfulness.The three giants turn around and start racing back down the mountain with their live takeaway.

‘What just happened?’ cries Rex. ‘What stopped him from eating Gilly? I’m getting a strong scent of tar, just like I smelt on Jack. There must be some still left on Gilly. Could that be why?’

‘Yes, I think so,’ replies Tommy Blue. ‘To giants, having tar on their grub is like us having earwax and pus rubbed on our food. Too horrible to eat. Thank goodness the twins’ parents couldn’t get it all off. It might have just saved her life.

‘Come on, Rex. If the giants travel through the secret gateway back home, Gilly will never be seen again – except as their main course! We’re not far from the top of the old slate quarry. If we can lead them there, we might have a chance of saving her and giving them a lesson they won't forget in a hurry.'

The quarry is situated near the top of the Skirrid and has been mined since Roman times. Roofs made with slate cut from deep within the mountainside can be seen, even today, across South Wales. The miners left this place a long time ago, and all that remains is a giant rip in the landscape.

The pit is over one hundred metres deep, with steep walls lined with large, sharp rocks, where very little grows except for a few brave shrubs.

Over time, water has come down the mountainside, creating a

magnificent lake that covers almost the entire pit floor. The slate surface has turned the icy water a lovely shade of aqua blue, which is so clear it's easy to see all the way to the bottom, many metres below. It's a beautiful but also a very dangerous place.

A thick forest of old oak trees stands all around the quarry, and many a visitor to the Skirrid has arrived suddenly at its cliff edge. Luckily, most of them have been saved from falling, but there have been some terrible accidents where people and their animals have landed in the icy waters, needing to be rescued.

'Rex,' says Tommy Blue, 'it's time I pressed the second button.'

CHAPTER 8

As Rex nods his head in agreement, Tommy Blue reaches towards the panel in front of him and presses a red, shiny button with the letter 'M' stamped on it.

The 'M' stands for 'magic'.

For a couple of seconds, nothing happens, and then with a flash of light, the chariot turns into a golden saddle that, with Tommy Blue safely strapped in place, sits on the back of a magnificent Welsh dragon.

Dear Reader, I did say that Rex could do more than talk. He can also, in times of great danger, when he and Tommy Blue need to move quickly and fight fearlessly, change into a dragon. A majestic and powerful winged beast who can fly at incredible speed and shoot out plumes of fire against his enemies.

Rex is truly breath-taking in his new form. Ten times larger than before and all black except for the mark on his head, which is now a real crown made from the same gold as the saddle.

He looks like a huge lizard, with four strong legs and two bat-like wings that arc folded by his side. His entire body is covered with an armour of thick, hard scales.

His mighty tail is curled and its tip, in the shape of a spearhead, points up towards the sky. He has spiky teeth, a long, pointed tongue, and razor-sharp claws. As he stands waiting for instructions from Tommy Blue, small curls of smoke puff out through his nostrils.

Tommy Blue reaches towards the control panel at the front of the saddle and switches on the

Giant Tracker. Looking closely, he watches as the giants move quickly down the side of the Skirrid. He can see that he and Rex need to lead them away from their current path and through the woods towards the quarry edge. His idea is to chase the giants over the cliff face so that they fall into the lake far below.

Timing is key, as they'll have to rescue Gilly before the giants hit the water's surface. If they get it wrong, Gilly will be in great danger. Luckily for Tommy Blue and Rex, giants are known to be rather stupid and easily distracted, two things the fearless friends are counting on for their plan to work.

They'll also need Nell's help. Tommy Blue whispers a secret spell, and a moment later the fairy arrives. Her golden hair lies in a long plait down her back, and she's dressed in a floor-length, red velvet dress.

Although she's very old, born when the world was new, she takes the form of a beautiful young woman. Around her neck is a pendant made from a small rock of Welsh gold, mined from deep within the earth. She's not alone. All around her are her loyal helpers, the Tatties.

The Tatties are funny little things. They look like baking potatoes the size of rugby balls. They each have two inky-black eyes, a long, straight mouth and a shock of green hair that sticks upwards like a carrot top.

With their short arms and legs and small, pretty hands, they're almost cute looking – apart from their oversized feet. These are long and thin with four big, ugly toes and sharp, claw-like nails.

It's because of their large feet that the Tatties can move so quickly. By gripping the ground with their toes, they can spring forward, taking great strides through the air as they run across the mountainside.

They live deep within the soil of the woodland, which they burrow into using their strong, bony toes. Safe and warm in their underground home, close to the resting place of their beloved Nell, they can sleep for weeks at a time. They may be small and funny looking, but they are brave fighters.

Nell turns her large, pale grey eyes to Tommy Blue.

‘What can I do to help you and Rex?’ she asks.

Tommy Blue tells her what’s happened before revealing his plan for rescuing Gilly, explaining that for it to work, Nell will need to change into her animal form.

‘Of course,’ she says before lowering her head and chanting a short spell.

Suddenly, there’s a rush of wind and smoke and Nell turns into a beautiful osprey, a striking bird of prey, dark brown with a white belly and face and over half a metre high.

Dear Reader, ospreys are eagle-eyed hunters with strong, taloned feet that are perfect for snatching fish out of rivers and lakes. They had been hunted to extinction in Wales, but they’re back now and their numbers are increasing rapidly.

A moment later, the osprey
and the dragon rise into the air,
beating their wings as one as they
soar majestically into the sky,
racing at great speed after the
giants.

CHAPTER 9

Tommy Blue loves the thrill of flying at speed. His hair blows wildly about his head as if it's dancing in delight. Rex and Nell fly like the wind, their wings beating rapidly, as they race to catch up with the giants.

They see the enemy running, and the quarry to their left. Battle ready, the fairy and Rex swoop down to their right. At first, the giants don't see them, then as Rex roars loudly and fires out a plume of red-hot flames, they turn around and gawp.

For a moment, they stand stock still, mouths open as they try to work out what's happening. Oda, the smartest of the three, is first to understand that they're under attack.

'Oi, you two!' she bellows at her brothers. 'It's that pesky dragon and rider again. We can't let them beat us. Don't you remember what happened last time? RUN!!!'

She spins around and starts racing off, away from the fire-breathing dragon and the osprey, followed by Ragnar and Rollo. In their panic, they can't move quickly enough, and Rex, getting closer, dives towards them. Then, when he's only a few metres away, he aims a jet of fire at Ragnar's large and warty bum.

The giant cries out in fear and pain as the flames hit their target. With Gilly still held tightly in his right hand, he frantically slaps out the sparks with his left.

'Follow me,' he screams at Oda and Rollo before charging off towards the woods.

As the three giants run as fast as they can from the dragon, they crash blindly through the landscape, uprooting trees and bushes in their path. Small animals cry out and scatter in fear, and birds rise from their now broken nests in clouds of ruffled feathers.

They swoop down at the giants, landing on their heads and

pecking madly until their enemies are running full pelt, mad with the need to escape.

The first part of the plan is working, and the giants are heading straight for the cliff edge. Now Tommy Blue and Rex need to save Gilly before Ragnar and the others fall into the quarry and land in the water below. They just have to get him to loosen his grip on the now screaming child.

The giants are moving fast, running for their lives. They are charging across the mountainside, unaware of what's ahead of them. The birds continue to attack them, blocking their view so that they can't see the danger ahead.

Then the Tatties join the chase. They move with great speed, and soon they're darting quickly between the legs of the giants, trying to trip them up. The army of tiny soldiers moves as one, making the ground look like water.

The giants stumble and it's not long before Oda falls. Her cry of pain as she loses her footing and lands face down on the ground causes the birds to stop their attack and fly away in panic. The speed and force of her massive bulk hitting the woodland floor sends out shock waves and causes Rex to flip upside down.

Tommy Blue starts to slip out of his seat.

‘Help!’ he shouts out in terror. ‘Rex, I don’t think I can hang on much longer.’

Just as it looks like all is lost and Tommy Blue is about to crash down into the woods below, Rex uses his superb flying skills and all his might to steer himself upright again.

Hurrah!!!

Tommy Blue and Rex are once again on track, chasing the brothers further through the woods. The osprey and the dragon beat their wings quickly to keep up the pace as Oda’s screams cause the other giants to run faster. She’s now covered in a moving blanket of Tatties, pinning her to the ground. Even in the face of the snakes, who writhe and hiss at them, they stay put, keeping Oda from her brothers.

'Gerroff me,' she shouts at them, trying to shake them off.

'You're hurting me.

'Let.

'Me.

'Go!'

Then, with a burst of energy, she lifts first her head and then her body off the ground.

Throwing off her attackers as she stands up, she runs to catch the others. The Tatties quickly jump up and race once more after the giants as they head towards the quarry edge.

Now comes the key – and most dangerous – part of the plan. Ragnar races blindly past the edge of the quarry and steps out into nothingness, his legs moving hopelessly as they try to find solid ground. Rex and the osprey see what's happened and dive into the quarry after him. Once they are flying alongside the giant, Nell swoops towards Rex, and with feet outstretched, she grabs the golden crown from his head. Once it is in her grasp, she turns towards Ragnar and throws it as hard as she can, aiming just in front of his face.

For a horrifying moment, Tommy Blue is sure that the plan has failed, and that Ragnar's mind is so full of escaping he hasn't seen the crown. Then suddenly, the giant moves his enormous, repulsive head in the direction of the glittering object and shouts out a cry of delight.

Dear Reader, giants love gold. They like to melt it in the fire pits near their swamps and use it to make rather ugly necklaces and earrings that they think bring out the beautiful yellow of their eyes. They also create toothpicks for picking the tiny bones of children out of their teeth.

Ragnar's eyes follow the crown as it flies past him, then, without thinking, he raises his right arm. As he grasps his prize, Gilly slips from his hand.

At the exact moment he seizes the crown, his face changes from glee to horror as he realises the gravity of the situation, and screams.

Rollo and Oda have also raced past the cliff edge, and now all three giants are falling and they, together with Gilly and the Tatties, are heading at speed towards the quarry floor.

As the giants flap their arms in a rather silly attempt at flight, the Tatties are not afraid. Their strange green hair starts spinning madly, causing them to hover in mid-air before they rise together, back up to the cliff edge. Once they're on solid ground, they stand close to the edge of the quarry, toes gripped into the earth, and watch.

Meanwhile, Tommy Blue and Rex race to save Gilly. Weaving through the falling giants, they manage to get ten metres under her. Any second now she will land safely on the saddle – but just at the moment she's about to be saved, Ragnar's left hand appears and snatches her away.

The giant, even as he falls towards a wet and painful landing, is thinking about lunch. But his triumph is short-lived as, with a loud thwack, he's hit from behind. Bellowing out in anger, he turns to see Rollo spinning round in mid-air, getting ready for a second punch.

'Give me the crown,' he screams as he hits Ragnar on the arm.

The older giant cries out in pain and loses his grip on his golden treasure. All three giants are clawing at the air, trying to get to the crown, but it's moving too fast and soon the giants are tumbled up together, heading at speed towards the cold, clear water below.

In the commotion, Ragnar's grip on Gilly weakens. Wriggling wildly and pushing with all her might at his large, smelly fingers, she manages to free herself.

As she falls through the air, Rex moves into position, and just a couple of metres above the lake, Gilly lands safely next to Tommy Blue. Immediately, Rex changes direction and soars skywards, away from danger.

Then disaster strikes.

Just as Tommy Blue is getting the straps in place to safely secure her, Gilly slips out of the saddle.

She falls towards a large rock sticking out from the quarry wall. As she lands on the hard surface, the sound of bones breaking and a scream of pain fill the air.

Tommy Blue and Rex race towards Gilly.

As they get nearer, they can see that something is very wrong.

The little girl is trying to stand, but her legs are shaking, and she looks very unsteady on her feet. She is obviously badly injured and she's ghostly white. Her right arm, the one she landed on, is hanging limply by her side.

Then, before Tommy Blue and Rex can get close to her, she stumbles and, with a cry, falls off the ledge and into the freezing water below.

CHAPTER 10

Rex doesn't need Tommy Blue to tell him what to do. He angles his powerful neck downwards, folding back his wings as his body cuts through the water's surface.

Tommy Blue just has time to pinch his nose and press his glasses into place before he's underwater.

Luckily, the water is so clear they soon spot Gilly sinking towards the bottom of the lake. Rex powers through the water, using his strong legs to swim quickly. He needs to get below Gilly before she hits the hard slate floor.

Faster and faster, he kicks until finally he's where he needs to be and Gilly lands once again on the saddle. Tommy Blue lets go of his nose and grabs hold of Gilly by her good arm, drawing her close to him as Rex rises through the water.

Crashing through the surface with a burst of spray, Rex heads towards the sky as Gilly and Tommy Blue

cough and splutter, taking great gulps of fresh air.

Below them, the giants splash down, one after the other, screaming in agony as they hit the water with force. They float on their backs, bobbing on the lake's surface. Soon pain turns to rage and all three roar with fury at being tricked out of a tasty morsel and a golden prize by Tommy Blue and Rex.

Dear Reader, do you know why the giants didn't sink? It's because they eat lots of slimy plants and grimy, pongy toads that they find near their swamp. They also eat their food far too quickly, so their tummies are full of rotting, stinky gas.

It's like us wearing armbands and rubber rings. The gas keeps them afloat. They really are quite revolting creatures. If you ever find yourself near one, make sure you're not downwind. Their farts are eye-wateringly nasty.

None of the giants are happy. Like all hideous monsters, they have a great fear of clean, fresh water. They spend hours every day in their swamp, soaking themselves in dirty goo. Giants fear the crystal-clear waters of the lake because they believe that having a layer of slime and mud on their skin keeps them strong and healthy. They're worried that if they wash it off, they will lose their mighty strength.

'*I've heard it said, it must be true, washing with water weakens you*' is seen roughly carved, and poorly spelt, into rotting tree stumps in every giant dwelling place. It's something they take very seriously.

As the giants kick and splash their way to the edge of the lake, filling the air with rude words and shouts of fury, our heroes make their escape.

'We did it, you're safe now, Gilly,' says Tommy Blue as he straps her into the saddle. Then, he turns to look at the little girl and sees with horror that she doesn't look well. She needs immediate medical care.

Tommy Blue presses the button shaped like a telephone and cries, 'Rex, Gilly's very poorly. We don't have a moment to lose. Nell is busy dealing with the giants and we're too far from any major road for an ambulance to get here quickly. We need to fly her to the hospital.'

Rex nods in agreement, and with a turn of his wings, the magnificent dragon heads away from the Skirrid towards Abergavenny and the hospital.

CHAPTER 11

As they fly towards the hospital, Tommy Blue looks back to the base of the quarry where he sees Nell appear on the narrow strip of land surrounding the lake, next to where the golden crown landed.

Changing back into her human form, she picks up the crown and brings her golden pendant to her lips. She whispers a spell, and the crown reappears on Rex's head.

It's not long before they arrive at the hospital and Rex lands in a small field nearby. Tommy Blue presses the button marked with the letter 'M' for the second time, and Rex is changed back into a dog. Still strapped into the chariot, with Tommy Blue and Gilly inside, Rex races at great speed to the entrance. Once there, he howls and howls until a doctor and three nurses run outside to see what's happening.

When she spots Gilly, the doctor swoops the little girl out of the chariot and holds her close as the others rush back inside to get a trolley. As soon as she's placed safely on a stretcher, Gilly is taken into the emergency room.

Moments later, one of the nurses reappears carrying a bowl of water for Rex and a can of fizzy cola for Tommy Blue.

He hands Tommy Blue his drink and places the bowl in front of Rex. Both take great gulps of their drinks – fighting giants and saving a little girl from a terrible fate is thirsty work!

'Will you two be OK out here on your own?' the nurse asks.

'Yes,' says Tommy Blue, 'but would you mind untying Rex please, so he can sit in the chariot with me?'

'Of course,' says the nurse.

As soon as the last strap is untied, Rex bounds into the chariot, snuggling close to Tommy Blue. Before he goes back inside the hospital, the nurse promises to see them as soon as he has news on Gilly.

Rex looks up at Tommy Blue and says, 'Well, thank goodness that's over. I was really scared for Gilly when she landed on that rock. I think she must have hurt herself quite badly. It was a good idea to fly her here. She's clearly in a lot of pain.'

'Yes, she is, but it could have been a lot worse,' replies Tommy Blue. 'Rex, your flying skills today were amazing. The way you dived into the lake to save Gilly was incredible. I'm so proud of you. Well done.' Tommy

Blue holds Rex close, stroking his back.

‘It was much harder than I thought it would be.’ says Rex. ‘As you know, I haven’t had to fly so fast and with such amazing grace and agility for a long time.’

Tommy Blue decides not to point out his chum’s bragging, because although it seems a bit rude to show off about your own successes, in this case, what Rex said was true.

‘It’s a good thing the water’s so clear there,’ continues Rex. ‘It was easy to see Gilly. And weren’t the Tatties great? Though I must say when they tripped up Oda I did think the shock waves would be our downfall. I could feel you slipping out of the saddle, and I was so scared you would fall to the ground.'

'Rex, we make a good team', says Tommy Blue as the two pals huddle tightly together.

They're almost nodding off, tired by their adventure, when, an hour later, the nurse comes back outside to see them. Holding Tommy Blue's hand, he tells them that Gilly is going to be all right.

'We've given her an X-ray, and she's broken her wrist. Her arm's in a plaster cast, big enough for all her friends to write on. She'll certainly be wanting your signature, Tommy Blue, and Rex's paw print. You two saved her life. She's told us what happened. You've all been very brave.

'She's had some medicine to make her feel better, and she's now sitting up in bed eating ice cream and jelly.'

He pats Rex on the head and then reaches into his rucksack for a biscuit for the dog and a slab of chocolate for Tommy Blue.

'I thought you both deserved a treat.'

Rex wolfs down the yummy biscuit, and Tommy Blue manages to bite off half the chocolate bar in one go. He smiles and thanks the nurse.

‘You’re both very welcome. Now, isn’t it time you two went home?’ he says. ‘Gilly is safe here. After a good night’s sleep, she’ll be well enough to go back to her family. I think the best thing you can do is let them know what’s happened. I’m sure they’re worried sick.’

‘Crickey,’ exclaims Tommy Blue. ‘You’re right. We need to get back to the villagers – they’ll be waiting for news.’

As there’s no time to lose, once the nurse has strapped Rex back into the chariot’s harness, Tommy Blue and Rex sprint back to the field next to the hospital.

Once there, far from the buildings, with plenty of space around them, Tommy Blue presses the magic button. In moments, the dragon and the boy are soaring back to the mountain and the Giant Shelter.

CHAPTER 12

Deep within the woods, the villagers are sheltering inside the cave that was used the last time they were visited by the giants. Created during the ice age, when the Skirrid itself was formed, this shelter has been a place of safety for centuries.

There's no better location for hiding from giants because its entrance is behind a towering and fast-flowing waterfall. Even if a giant realises there are children behind the water, they wouldn't walk to the cave's entrance for fear of getting wet. Once they're inside, the villagers know they are safe from attack.

Mr Jones has lit a fire. As Giant Warden, one of his main jobs is to make sure that there is always a supply of logs in the cave, along with enough food and drink to last a couple of days.

He's built a huge bonfire near the entrance and it is roaring, keeping everyone warm. Flames are shooting up to the ceiling of the cave, and the villagers are gathered around it, grateful for the heat it brings.

Mum is busy using a long metal fork to toast slices of bread, which Dad spreads with loads of lovely fresh, Welsh butter before handing them out to the children. They are worried about Tommy Blue and Rex, but they know it's important to look after the others.

Dear Reader, are you kind like Tommy Blue's parents? I'm sure you are. Kindness is a very special thing. It costs nothing and can be as simple as a smile, a gentle word, or a hug, but the effect it can have on someone is truly magical – even more magical than Rex.

As the children eat their tasty snack, the butter melts and they have to use the backs of their hands to wipe their greasy chins.

The youngsters are having lots of fun, laughing and joking with one another around the campfire. One of the older girls has brought a joke book called *Corny Laffs*, and the children take it in turns to read out jokes.

'I've got a good one,' says one of the boys. 'What do you call a cat that walks across the desert on Christmas Day?'

The children spend a minute thinking what the answer might be, then give up.

'Dunno,' replies one. 'What?'

The boy starts to titter, and it takes him a moment to get the answer out.

‘It’s Sandy Claws, of course. Get it? Sandy Claws – Santa Claus.’

All the children start to laugh. All, that is, except for one of the younger boys who needs his sister to explain it, and when he understands the joke, he bursts into such a violent fit of giggles that he accidentally farts loudly. This causes all the children to shriek even more in delighted disgust.

Only Jack is quiet. He is snuggled close to his mum as she stands with his dad and some of the other parents away from the fire, near the back of the cave. They are talking quietly, wondering how Tommy Blue and Rex are getting on.

‘How long has it been now?’ asks Gilly’s mum nervously. ‘It seems like ages.’

‘It’s only five minutes since you last asked, my darling’ says her husband gently. ‘Try not to worry,’ he says, pulling his wife and Jack into a tight bear hug. ‘Tommy Blue and Rex have saved us from the giants before and I’m sure they’ll do so again. We just need to be patient.’

Suddenly, one of the adults yells, ‘I think I can hear something. It sounds like the beat of giant wings. It might be Rex in his dragon form.’

Wooosh, wooosh!

Mr Jones runs outside and peers around the edge of the waterfall, searching the sky for any sign of the dragon.

CHAPTER 13

With a sudden swoop, the dragon appears and dives through the curtain of water, landing gracefully on the ledge outside the cave entrance.

Folding his wings, he lowers himself down onto the ground, and the Giant Warden runs up to Tommy Blue.

'What's happened?' he shouts. 'Where's Gilly? Are you and Rex OK?'

'Gilly's in hospital. She's hurt her arm but she's going to be fine,' says Tommy Blue. 'Rex and I are good, thanks. It was a bit scary, but we fought bravely and defeated the giants. Nell and the Tatties are taking them back to the Land of the Giants now. It's over, Mr Jones. Please can you let everyone know Gilly's safe? Then tell them to get their stuff and come outside. It's time to get them home.'

As the old man goes back into the cave, Tommy Blue presses the magic button and Rex becomes a dog once more, pulling the chariot with Tommy Blue safely inside. Gilly's family are first to come out, with Mum and Dad close behind. Tommy Blue tells them what's happened. Jack whoops with delight and runs to his mother and father, who hold him close.

‘Thank goodness she’s safe. I can’t thank you two enough for saving my beautiful girl,’ says the twins’ dad, his eyes full of tears.

Mum runs up to Tommy Blue and gives him a hug and a big, fat kiss on the cheek.

‘Well done, my brave boy,’ she says. ‘And you, Rex.’

Soon, all the villagers are outside, and once they’ve walked along the ledge behind the waterfall to the open mountainside, Tommy Blue and Rex lead them home.

Spirits are high and as they walk towards the village, they sing an ancient folk song in Welsh that tells the tale of when, centuries ago, dragons first came to

Wales. They're all feeling tired, but happy and excited to have escaped once again from the giants.

***

Meanwhile, back in the quarry, Nell gets to work using powerful spells to place the giants into a deep sleep. She's spent the time Tommy Blue and Rex have been at the hospital checking on her Tattie army. Luckily, none have been hurt in the fighting.

Now, she lifts the three giants two metres above the water's surface and uses special golden thread to bind them together. Then she raises her pendant, quietly murmurs a spell, and the giants, fairy, and Tatties disappear.

They next appear deep inside the woods, not far from where Tommy Blue is leading the villagers home. This is where the portal to the Land of the Giants lies. The gateway is in the trunk of a huge rowan tree, heavy with fire-red berries. Nell lets the giants drop onto the ground. Despite the rough landing, they're all still fast asleep, no longer a threat to anyone.

CHAPTER 14

Working quickly, Nell opens the gateway that the giants had sealed behind them, using a string of powerful spells. She's about to throw the three giants through the portal when Ragnar wakes with a start.

Like all giants, he is not a naturally quick thinker, but even he understands what's happening and, more importantly, that he's lost his lunch. Shaking off the golden thread that's wrapped around him, he jumps up with surprising speed and agility for someone so huge.

Taking the fairy by surprise, he pushes her roughly through the portal, where she lands in a heap on the floor of the other world. Crowing with delight at the thought of a tasty snack, the giant gallops away, following his nose towards the scent of human children. As Nell stands up and starts to make her way back through the rowan trunk, the Tatties spring into action.

They race together at great speed towards Ragnar. They have to move fast, quicker than they ever have before, to catch and trip him up before he snatches and eats one of the children. The villagers are close by. The giant can hear the high voices of the children in song, and his stomach gurgles loudly.

Immediately, the singing stops. Although they can't see him, everyone can sense that something has gone wrong and somehow one or all the giants have escaped, and are close by. Some of the children start to cry and their parents hold them tight, whispering soft words to them as they try to keep them calm.

Mr Jones moves quickly to the back of the group, ready to return them to the shelter as Tommy Blue and Rex race up the bank that borders the road, in the dirction of the giant's rumbling tummy.

The Tatties dash along the woodland floor, but it's no good – Ragnar's moving too fast, and soon he's near the road the villagers are travelling home along. He is seconds away from coming face to face with our heroes and the children, and the thought of what he might do to them all in temper and hunger is horrifying.

Then, just as Tommy Blue and Rex reach the top of the bank, Nell appears before the giant, causing him to come to a dead stop. She is magnificent in her anger, ten times her normal size and with the face and body of an old and terrifying witch. Hovering in the air, eye to eye

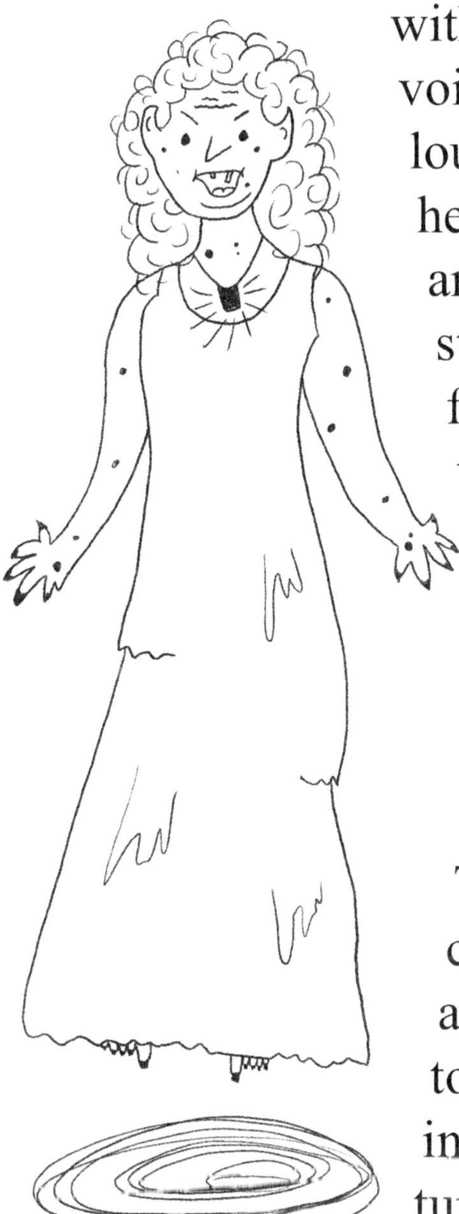

with the giant, her voice is strong and loud as she points her pendant at him and calls out a stunning spell. The force of it knocks the giant off his feet, and he falls backwards, landing with a deafening thud on the floor.

The impact causes the little army of Tatties to rise a metre into the air before tumbling back to earth. Landing in a tangle of feet and hair, they quickly separate before, at Nell's command, they line up along the length of the giant and, using their powerful feet, roll him back to where his brother and sister are still asleep.

Tommy Blue and Rex breathe a sigh of relief as they watch their monstrous foe being defeated, and they rush back to tell the villagers what happened.

Everyone shouts out three cheers when they hear the news and head home once more. Mr Jones, walking at the front alongside Tommy Blue and Rex, starts singing a funny song, and soon the sound of laughter and music fills the air.

By the time they all return to the village, they're pleased and very relieved to be safe once more. Waving goodbye to the villagers as they let themselves back into their homes, the Blue family head towards Dad's van. As soon as Tommy Blue and Rex are safely inside, they set off back to the farmhouse, towing the chariot behind them.

'Look,' says Mum as they pass the twins' house. 'They're going straight to see Gilly. I don't blame them. They'll want to see their little girl tonight. They were all worried sick. I've never known Jack be so quiet.'

Then, she turns around to look at Tommy Blue and Rex.

‘I’m so proud of you both,’ she says. ‘What you two did today was amazing. You’re the best boy, and dog, in all the whole world.’

‘Hear, hear,’ says Dad. ‘Now let’s get home.’

REX
DAD
MUM

CHAPTER 15

At the rowan tree, Nell, back to her human form, uses spells to carry the bodies of the sleeping giants through the gateway before closing the entrance.

She builds in more magical spells than before, making it as safe as possible. Nobody wants to let the giants come back a third time, causing more chaos and danger.

Finally, she ties a chain, heavy with charms of woodland animals and flowers, around the tree. This should be unbreakable and will hopefully stop Ragnar and the other giants coming through the portal again.

When she's finished casting her spells, Nell and her Tatties return to their home by an old and gnarled oak tree. As she lies down under a pile of soft leaves, her helpers bury into the ground around her and fall fast asleep. Nell knows she can return to her slumber, safe in the knowledge that Tommy Blue and Rex will be there to guard the mountain.

***

Back at the farmhouse, Tommy Blue and Rex are in the kitchen. Mum made sure that Tommy Blue had a nice hot bath when he got home, and he's now sitting at the table, dressed in his pyjamas and dressing gown, pink-cheeked from the heat and excitement.

Next to him, Rex is glowing from a good brushing and lots of kisses and cuddles from Mum. Tommy Blue's parents have spent the last twenty minutes quizzing him, wanting to know everything that happened, and they've finally run out of steam and questions.

'Well,' says Mum as she gets up and stretches, 'I don't know about you lot, but I'm worn out. What we all need is a strong cup of tea and a slice of cake. Tommy Blue, do you want some?'

'You bet,' says Tommy Blue, 'and please can Rex have a

slice too? And don't cut small portions, Mum, we're starving. Make them gigantic!'

And with that, Tommy Blue and Rex start to laugh and laugh, and the sound of their laughter travels across the mountainside.

Relief and happiness have once more descended on the Skirrid. The school holidays have officially started, and there's a haircut and a bag of sweets to look forward to tomorrow. Life is back to normal, and it feels like everything will be peaceful forever more – or at least until the next Tommy Blue and Rex adventure!

***

Dear Reader, I hope you enjoyed this story of Tommy Blue and Rex. You'll be pleased to learn that the doctors and nurses were so impressed by the speed our two heroes got Gilly to them that all hospitals in Wales and the rest of the United Kingdom now have special air ambulance helicopters.

They're not as exciting as Rex in his dragon form, but like him, they get ill people to hospital very quickly. So next time you hear something flying high above you, look up. It might be one of these helicopters – or it could be a magnificent Welsh dragon called Rex.

Until the next time I see you, goodbye and good luck, or as we say in Wales, hwyl fawr a phob lwc.

AUTHOR PROFILE

After retiring from a 30-year career in the civil service, Jane Carter joined a local writing group in January 2020. She started writing poetry and flash fiction, with some publishing success, before moving on to writing stories for children.

Tommy Blue and Rex in Gigantic Danger was the first story she wrote and was shortlisted in the 2022 Firefly Competition.

Jane spent her early years in Abergavenny and now lives in Caerleon with her family.

WHAT DID YOU THINK OF TOMMY BLUE AND REX IN GIGANTIC DANGER?

A big thank you for purchasing this book. It means a lot that you chose this book specifically from such a wide range on offer. I do hope you enjoyed it.

Book reviews are incredibly important for an author. All feedback helps them improve their writing for future projects and for developing this edition. If you are able to spare a few minutes to post a review on Amazon, that would be much appreciated.

PUBLISHER INFORMATION

rowanvale
books

Rowanvale Books provides publishing services to independent authors, writers and poets all over the globe. We deliver a personal, honest and efficient service that allows authors to see their work published, while remaining in control of the process and retaining their creativity. By making publishing services available to authors in a cost-effective and ethical way, we at Rowanvale Books hope to ensure that the local, national and international community benefits from a steady stream of good quality literature.

For more information about us, our authors or our publications, please get in touch.

www.rowanvalebooks.com
info@rowanvalebooks.com

Printed in Great Britain
by Amazon

49067208R00071